The Princess and the Tree

For Luca Anholt, with Seriously Silly wishes L.A.

For Abigail, with love A.R.

Visit Laurence Anholt's website at www.anholt.co.uk

ORCHARD BOOKS
338 Euston Road
London NW1 3BH
Orchard Books Australia
Level 17/207 Kent Street, Sydney, NSW 2000

First published by Orchard Books in 2009

Text © Laurence Anholt 2009
Illustrations © Arthur Robins 2009

The rights of Laurence Anholt to be identified as the author
and of Arthur Robins to be identified as the illustrator
of this work have been asserted by them in accordance
with the Copyright, Designs and Patents Act, 1988.

A CIP catalogue record for this book is available from the British Library.

ISBN 978 1 84616 080 6 (hardback)
ISBN 978 1 84616 319 7 (paperback)

1 2 3 4 5 6 7 8 9 10 (hardback)
4 5 6 7 8 9 10 (paperback)

Printed in China

Orchard Books is a division of Hachette Children's Books,
an Hachette UK company.
www.hachette.co.uk

Laurence Anholt Arthur Robins

seriously SILLY colour

The Princess and the Tree

ORCHARD BOOKS

There was once a naughty Prince.
He was always mucking about
with his mate, Silly Willy the jester.

Silly Willy and the Prince rode their bikes around the castle and got into all kinds of mischief . . .

BANG! CLANG! CRASH!

They made so much racket that
no one could get any peace at all.

It drove the King and Queen
barmy.

Silly Willy and the Prince hated
going to bed. They stayed up all
night pumping out loud rap music.
Their favourite singer was the
Razzle Dazzle Rap Princess . . .

"Some of us have to work for
a living," shouted the King.

Early in the morning, when everyone else was getting up, the Prince and Silly Willy crept into their beds and slept all day long.

"It's time he found a nice princess and got a palace of his own," said the King.
They put up advertisements in every corner of the kingdom . . .

WANTED
Princess to marry noisy Prince.
Must be able to sleep through
ANYTHING!

It wasn't long before a queue
of princesses turned up at
the palace.
Some were tall, some were tiny.
Some were poor, some were posh.

The Queen made lovely soft beds
for each princess, but the minute
they fell asleep, Silly Willy and the
Prince would pump up the volume,
and the poor princesses would run
screaming into the night . . .

BOOM, BOOM, BOOM!
I must confess,
I'm better than the best.
I'm the Rap Princess!

The King and Queen thought they
would never get any peace at all.

One night there was a terrible storm. The wind and rain blew around the palace and lightning flickered in the sky.
Silly Willy and the Prince thought it was brilliant!

The poor old King and Queen
had even less sleep than usual.
First there was thunder, and
then a huge tree blew down in
the palace garden . . .
KERR-RASH!
Finally somebody started ringing
the doorbell very loudly.

The King went downstairs in
his pyjamas.
A mysterious stranger stood on
the doorstep, dressed in black
and dripping with water.

I was ridin' my bike
in the rain and the storm.
I said, "That cosy castle
sure looks warm."

"Oh," said the King. "I suppose
you'd better come in."
"You can bring your bike inside
like we do," giggled Silly Willy.

So the mysterious rider rode up
the steps and into the hall.
BRR-OOO-MM!

"We'll make you a lovely soft bed," said the Queen.
"But you won't get much sleep around here," warned the King, "what with the storm and these two mucking about . . ."

"Well," said the King, "If you can sleep one night in this place you can marry our son."

19

The Queen put the stranger in
a huge warm bed with lots of
mattresses.
She was so tired, she didn't
even take off her helmet.
In two seconds she was fast
asleep and snoring gently.

The Prince and Silly Willy were worried. They went downstairs and played their music AS LOUDLY AS THEY COULD . . .

BOOM, BOOM, BOOM!
He's my King.
Razzle dazzle,
He's got loadsa bling!

But still the stranger kept snoring.

Silly Willy and the Prince pushed
the bed out of the bedroom.
And still she kept on snoring.

Along the landing and down
the stairs . . .

out of the door
and into the storm . . .

down a hill and along the river . . .

up the stairs and into
the bedroom . . .

And still she kept on snoring.
"It's that big soft bed," puffed the
Prince. "It's far too comfortable."

Then Silly Willy had an idea.
He ran outside and came
back with the huge tree
from the garden!

24

They lifted the sleeping stranger
and put the tree under the
bottom mattress.

But still she kept on snoring.

By morning, the Prince and
Silly Willy were exhausted.

At last the mysterious stranger
came down the stairs.

The Prince and
Silly Willy couldn't
believe their eyes . . .

"Goodness!" said the King.
"And how did you sleep?"
asked the Queen.

There was thunder and rain,
and wind and fog.
But I didn't hear nothin'
cos I slept like a LOG!

29

And they were tree-mendously happy for the rest of their silly lives.

Vrrooooooom!

ENJOY ALL THESE SERIOUSLY SILLY STORIES!

All priced at £4.99

Orchard books are available from all good bookshops, or can be ordered direct from the publisher:
Orchard Books, PO BOX 29, Douglas IM99 1BQ
Credit card orders please telephone: 01624 836000 or fax: 01624 837033
or visit our website: www.orchardbooks.co.uk or e-mail: bookshop@enterprise.net for details.

To order please quote title, author and ISBN and your full name and address.
Cheques and postal orders should be made payable to 'Bookpost plc.'
Postage and packing is FREE within the UK (overseas customers should add £1.00 per book).

Prices and availability are subject to change.